With thanks to the Preschool Camp and the Learning Center
at the Claudio Marzollo Community Center of Philipstown, N.Y.
— J.M.

With thanks to Polly Townsend and
the Desmond-Fish Library's Parent / Child Workshop
— W.W.

ISBN 978-0-545-41583-5

I Spy Animals was originally published as a board book
under the title *I Spy Little Animals*.

Text copyright © 1998 by Jean Marzollo.
"Creepy Crawly Cave," "Mirror Maze," "Prizes to Win," and "Puppet Theater" from
I Spy Fun House © 1993 by Walter Wick; "Chain Reaction," "The Hidden Clue,"
"The Mysterious Monster," and "The Toy Box Solution" from *I Spy Mystery* © 1993
by Walter Wick; "Clouds," "The Deep Blue Sea," and "Yikes!" from *I Spy Fantasy* © 1994
by Walter Wick; "Storybook Theater" from *I Spy School Days* © 1995 by Walter Wick.
All Published by Scholastic Inc.

22 21 20   ·   18 19 20 21 22

Printed in the U.S.A.   40 • This edition first printing, January 2012

I SPY
ANIMALS

Rhymes by Jean Marzollo

Photographs by Walter Wick

Cartwheel
·B·O·O·K·S·®

SCHOLASTIC INC.
New York Toronto London Auckland
Sydney Mexico City New Delhi Hong Kong

I spy

a bird

and a small balloon.

I spy

a turtle

and a little spoon.

I spy

a horse

and a yellow duck.

I spy

an elephant

and a zebra truck.

I spy

a bike

and a dog with a hat.

I spy

a fire hydrant

and a kitty cat.

I spy  a horse

and a little red car.

I spy

a door

and a starfish star.

I spy

a fish

and a yellow dog.

I spy

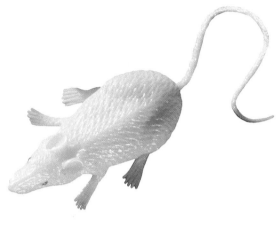

a mouse

and a spotted frog.

I spy

a duck,

a phone,

a tree.

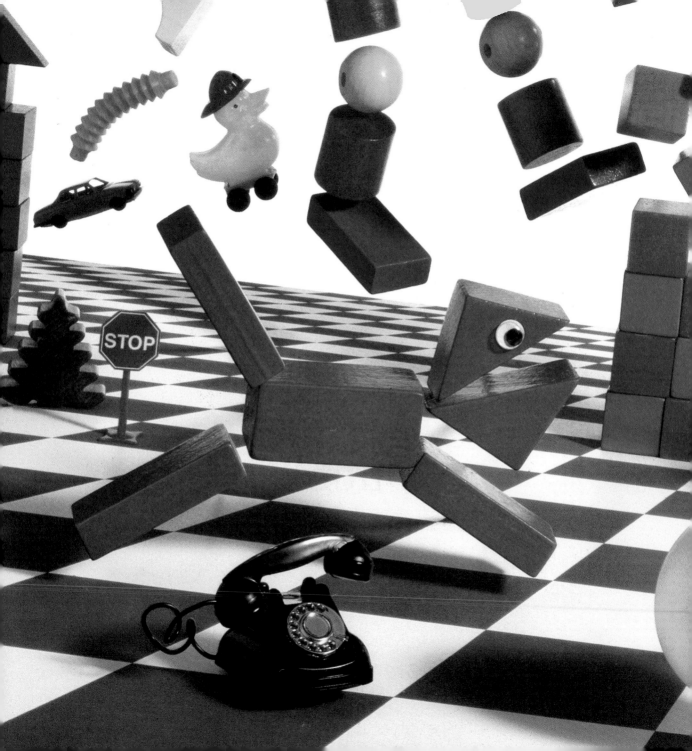

I spy

a bunny rabbit

just for me!

When you are done, go back and look...

rabbit

two fish

panda with a ball

What else can you find in your I Spy book?

leopard

lizard

lamb

Collect the I Spy books

Classics

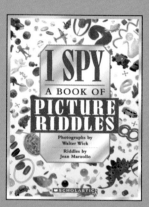

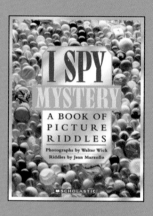

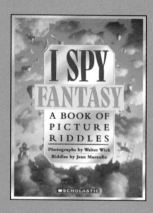

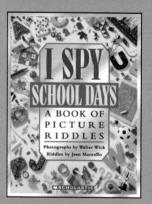

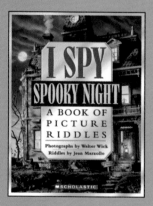

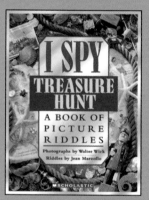

Collect the I Spy books

Challengers

 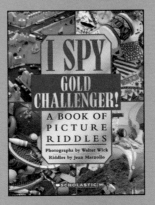 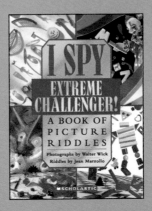

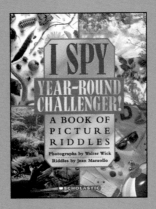 

Also available are *I Spy A to Z*, *I Spy Spectacular*, I Spy early readers, I Spy Little board books, and *I Spy Phonics Fun*.

Find all the I Spy books and more at www.scholastic.com/ispy/.